A CRACK

in the sidewalk

Suzanne Mason

ISBN: 978-0-9818597-5-0

Book layout and cover design by Christine Davanzo
Printed in the United States of America

First Edition

For Ernie

A Crack in the Sidewalk

The long shadows of late afternoon moved faster than the folks who lived there. During the summer months, neighbors said it was so hot you could fry eggs on the sidewalk. I never saw that theory tested, but the notion was always curious to me whenever I thought of home.

I stared out the limousine window. Doubt crept into my thoughts as I remembered the fast-paced touring schedule, media commitments, and public relations photo ops. Constant reminders of professional deadlines echoed through my mind. I didn't hear the applause anymore. The joy of my music was evaporating.

I never felt like part of the elite, but I did feel like one of the lucky ones. In spite of the long hours of practice, rehearsals, and fitful sleep in hotel rooms and airplanes, I was happy living my childhood dream of sharing my music with the world. Except that lately the dream had become a nightmare—the passion and delight in my music was riddled with frustration and self-doubt, and I was floundering. Most of the time I didn't know what city I was in, and lately I didn't care. Until today.

The limousine slowly circled the gazebo and turned down Comal Street. Pecan trees lined the street with Spanish moss hanging from the limbs like an old man's beard. I inched forward on the car seat. "The house is on the left," I said, "You can't miss it. It's the only Victorian on the block." *If I'm not too late*, I thought, fearful I was about to discover my treasure lost.

Years ago, the most congested traffic circling the gazebo was the children's Fourth of July pet parade. It was one of those fried-eggs-on-the-sidewalk days, the heat bearing down like an anvil. In spite of the lively beat of the marching band, those of us in the parade—the majority under the age of six—moseyed down the street with a menagerie of bored animals, fidgeting and looking in all directions with little attention paid to the task at hand. In most cases, loosely-held leashes dragged on the ground—evidence of our feeble attempts to keep dogs, piglets, goats and a pony in line. If any of us had an itch to scratch, we scratched it, and the leash would slip out of our grasp. As animals escaped, screams and laughter ensued as they ran wild among band members, children, and parade watchers. While a few industrious grown-ups attempted to corral the herd, they quickly realized the insanity of such efforts and instead joined the chorus of howls and laughter. It was total chaos, and the best pet parade we'd ever had.

It was a whisper of a town that was born inside of me before I was born—a place that continued to take on a life of its own with ease and without my permission after I'd left. On quiet nights after a performance in an unfamiliar city, with all the audience members on their way home, I sometimes found myself envious of all my hometown's residents. After traveling all over the world, I understood there was nowhere else on earth I could have been born.

I was almost home, but still questioned my decision to come here. The house had been empty for years and I'd heard recently that it had been condemned. As I pondered what I might see, I suddenly realized the car wasn't moving. I looked up, and held my breath. "I'm home," I whispered, my heart pounding with anticipation.

I got out of the car and mumbled a thank you to the driver. I took a few steps toward the house when my heel was caught in a crack in the sidewalk. I reached down to retrieve it and felt as if my hand was being pulled deeper into the crack. I finally grabbed my shoe and pulled it free, taking it off my foot in the process. I removed my other shoe and held them both in my hand as I stood tall and listened to the chatter of leaves in the breeze. *I will find myself. I will reclaim my love of music.* The thought was clear and calm. Maybe it was even a prayer.

I walked to the pecan tree in the middle of the front yard and sat down underneath as memories flooded toward me. I took a deep breath as I slowly examined every inch of my childhood home. Honeysuckle vines wrapped around the columns of the front porch and sweetened the haze like bits of sugar in a glass of iced tea. The house looked as if it had been freshly painted, and the porch swing—a haven on rainy days amidst daydreams and paper dolls—was intact. Half a dozen ferns hung the length of the front porch, the fronds cascading to the floor like a green waterfall. Caught by the breeze, the feather-like fronds moved about as if swaying to the rhythm of an orchestra.

I rested my head against the tree trunk, closed my eyes, and drifted back in time. I thought of the front window seat, where I took small breaks between hours of violin practice. I smiled and remembered summer afternoons when the temptation was great for a game of hide and seek with brothers, cousins, and playmates.

"You can't hide from me!"

I sat up, startled to see a little girl running across the lawn, stopping dead in her tracks when she saw me. She looked to be about 9 years old—a small child with delicate features, cheeks flush with excitement, freckles sprinkled across her nose. Someone had attempted to tie her blonde hair away from her face, but both the ribbon and her hair hung loosely down her back. I recognized her immediately.

She put her hands on her hips and asked, "Who are you?", in a tone meant to imply that I was the intruder—sitting on her special spot under the tree, no less. I was sure of the answer, but unsure how to respond. She waited, determined to stand tall until I gave her an answer.

"Uh, I'm a friend of your mother's."

"My mom told me not to talk to strangers," she said with authority.

"I'm not a stranger." She relaxed her hands to her sides and in almost a whisper asked, "Do you know me?" She turned her head slightly and looked at me as if she was examining a puzzle. She was!

"I've known you all my life."

“What's your name?"

"My name is Katherine."

"That's my name, but my friends call me Kate." She stepped closer—close enough for me to linger hopelessly in her liquid brown eyes. I didn't want to frighten her and waited until she decided it would be all right to continue our conversation.

"My mom's in the house. Do you want me to get her?"

"No, I'd really like to talk to you," I said.

"W-e-l-l," she hesitated as I held my breath.

"My mom's in the house.” She glanced over her shoulder at the house and then looked back at me. “I guess it'll be okay." She relaxed.

"Why don't you sit down so we can talk?”

"About what?" She asked, as she plopped down and rested her head against the tree trunk. I inhaled deeply as tears welled up in my eyes. Kate was so close that I could reach out and touch her, but I dared not.

"Do you live here?"

"Uh, huh."

"Are you happy?"

"Yes!" She sat up and looked at me. I regained my

composure and pushed back my tears, hoping she hadn't noticed.

"What do you like to do besides play hide and seek?" Her eyes lit up. "I like to play my violin. Nobody else in my school plays the violin as good as me," giggling as she talked.

"Why do you play?"

"Because I make it sound pretty, and it's fun, and...." She looked away from me as if embarrassed.

"Do you love it, Kate? Really love it?"

"Yes. It makes me happy." She looked at me again and smiled. *If I could only feel the joy and passion that she felt!* I wanted to capture her enthusiasm and pack it inside my heart so deeply that I could carry it with me wherever I traveled.

"I know it makes you happy, I can tell, but—do you get tired of playing?"

"Sometimes," she said matter-of-factly.

"What do you do then?"

"I stop, but then I miss it and start playing again."

"You have a gift."

"I guess." She pulled her knees up under her chin and played with the blades of grass between her toes.

"One day people will come to hear you play."

"How do you know that?" She looked at me and frowned with her question.

"I just have a feeling." *There is so much I want to tell you.*

"Mmmmm." Her frown softened and she said, "It'll be like when I played in my recital. It was fun, but I was nervous."

"That's okay, sometimes I get nervous too." *Like this very minute.*

"Where did you come from?" It was another question I struggled with, because how could I respond and make sense of it? I hedged a bit, biding my time, hoping maybe a thunderous bolt would strike and fill me with all the answers. But my mind kept going around in circles, looking for clues that would help this make sense. I made an attempt to respond as well as I could.

"Well, more important than that, I need to figure out where I'm going." Suddenly, she jumped up and said, "I know where we can go!"

"Where?" *I would follow you anywhere.*

"Follow me!", she yelled as she ran down the driveway and disappeared into the backyard. I knew exactly where I would find her—the home base swing set. It was the congregation spot for secret-telling and grave decisions, such as who would hide and who would count, and, for me, a solitary spot where many a daydream was concocted. She was waiting in the swing, just as I knew she would be.

"Push me! Push me!"

"You don't need me to push you, Kate. You can do it without my help."

"I know, I know. Just give me one push. That's all I

need. I can do the rest myself." *You are right.*

"I want to go high!" *Oh, you will.*

I stood behind her and pushed, but cautioned, "Be careful. You might fall."

"I won't fall. I like to go high!" She glided through the air like a trapeze artist. "I can see everything from here. I'm flying!"

"Hold on Kate. You're going too high, too fast."

"It's f-u-n." *Was it?*

"Come on. You can do it too!" she encouraged breathlessly. *I don't know if I can.*

"Don't be afraid!" *But I am.*

Kate went higher and higher. I envied her spirit and inched closer to the other swing. The rush of air I felt as she flew by enticed me to grab it and sit down. I pushed off the ground and pumped back and forth until all but the treetops blurred. My skirt whipped in the wind like my mother's linens hung out to dry on a summer afternoon.

Kate was right, it was like flying, and I had forgotten. The momentum pushed me forward toward the moon, which was nearing the horizon and felt just out of reach. Daydreams and memories, harbored in the late afternoon light, were aroused. I thought of the long afternoon shadows that moved across the yard when I was a young girl, marking the hours of music lessons and practice. I remembered running home from school for the best part of the day, when I was free to play my music, and the hush that fell in the house after every practice, so similar to the way the chatter of an audience always settles down to a whisper right before a concert begins. I heard the sound of laughter and suddenly realized it was me.

I flexed my feet and pumped harder, stretching my toes until they ached. "I'm touching the m-o-o-n!", I howled. And in that instant I knew: *Everything will be alright.*

Cradled in the smooth rhythm of the swing, I leaned back and drifted on the breeze, thinking of Kate. Even knowing what lay ahead for her—the long nights on the road, the bone-numbing fatigue—I was also in awe of her boldness. I knew she would make it on her own terms; I knew she would do it her own way. I wanted to tell her that as long as she remembered the passion and joy—the reason she chose music above all else—it would all be worth it in the end.

I jumped off the swing feeling giddy, anticipating another game. As I landed, a sudden burst of wind kicked up a spiral of dust that traveled past the swingset and disappeared around the corner of the house. I looked around for Kate, but she was nowhere to be seen. After a moment I understood, and laughed out loud.

“Are we playing hide and seek now? You can't hide from me!" I shouted, running to the front yard. As soon as I saw the pecan tree, I stopped. Particles of dust burned my eyes. I rubbed them as the wind died down, and then blinked as everything settled. Suddenly I understood; I could see clearly now.

Broken window panes were scattered across the yard. The porch swing had collapsed on one side and was hanging by a rusty chain. The baskets of ferns were gone. Tiny chips of paint lay scattered on the porch like confetti, peeled and fallen after years of neglect. Where there were once bluebonnets and coneflowers, weeds had taken over. Street lights flickered on in the distance as a star sailed across the sky. It was a celebration of my homecoming, and of Kate. Joy filled my heart, and I smiled.

I traced

my face

with my

fingertips.

It is still

foreign

territory.

Opal Mae's Cafe

The traffic light is located at the top of the hill near the old cotton mill. Opal Mae's Cafe is located in the center of town. Nobody remembers when the traffic light was put up, but everybody remembers back when Opal Mae's first opened. The memory of the town is short when it comes to the traffic light. The memory of the town is long when it comes to Opal Mae's Café. Five years ago the traffic light broke down because it snowed and nobody knew how to fix it. Opal Mae's is open no matter the weather. Why, back after the hurricane in 2013 she opened her doors even though part of her sign blew off and landed on the front porch of the only all female organization in town. There it was as big as you please: Specialty—Fresh Tarts. We haven't had a hurricane since then and nobody knows how to fix the traffic light because Leroy programmed the darn thing and then ran off with Sheriff Hilmer's daughter. Sheriff Hilmer sat at the counter in Opal Mae's Café on Sunday morning reading the newspaper. Euna Louise and Juna Louise Finch joined him and ordered their usual stuffed pork chops with mashed potatoes, extra gravy, and double biscuits with honey on the side. Opal Mae told the Finch girls that throughout all the years they'd been coming to the cafe it was obvious how they had grown together. I think it was Euna who thanked her. Juna asked if we'd heard the ruckus Saturday night coming from the house or seen the activity that commenced to the front lawn. She went on to say that in the midst of Iona's tricks of the trade, one of her bald-headed customers ran out of the house yelling and screaming and chasing her all over the front lawn because in the heat of their activity she caught his toupee on fire with her flaming batons. Juna spoke in a whisper as we all leaned in closer, but loud enough for everyone to hear. Juna said that the ceilings in that house aren't high enough for baton twirling and Iona should surely be enough familiar with what she observed looking from her usual reclined position. Juna continued and said she had to give Iona credit though since she stayed by her brother Buddy's side day and night after the backhoe incident. Why, she wheeled him right up to the front of the revival meeting last summer and Reverend Gaddis's eyes nearly popped out. Euna said had it not been for the bad blood between her and Reverend Gaddis when the Silver Spur Mobile Home Park burned down, she would have considered his proposal of marriage. Juna looked at Euna like she had lost her marbles and told her she had lost her marbles. She went on to say that Reverend Gaddis's eyebrows never did grow back after the fire and his head looked more like a bowling ball than it did before the fire, and he was drinking so heavily back then he surely didn't know which one he was proposing to—Euna or Juna. Opal Mae cleared her throat and changed the subject. She asked if we remembered when they put up the pedestrian mall where the Silver Spur Mobile Home Park used to be and how much trouble they had attracting customers because of all the white goo underfoot. She reminded us that the city council gave Buddy the mission of driving the starlings away and that he experimented with all sorts of gadgets for weeks on end. Juna said she remembered him beating the tree trunks with big sticks for three days and nights and then came down with repetitive stress syndrome. She went on to say that Buddy made that mechanical owl and rigged it to light up and make noise, but that irritated everybody in town for all the racket. And then he found those crackling balls over in Purl County. Opal Mae laughed and said it was a sight to behold, watching Buddy shoot his plastic balls up into the trees and lighting up the night sky like fireworks on the Fourth of July. Dogs were still howling three days later. Euna asked Opal Mae for a piece of chocolate cake and Opal Mae asked if she was sure she wanted cake or would she prefer apple pie. Juna reminded Opal Mae that they never did prove that her waitresses had anything to do with the cake incident when they all celebrated over at the community hall last year. Opal Mae said she supposed it turned out to be all right since they added more bathroom facilities after the incident. Euna said that Iona did try and establish herself in a new career, as we all should remember back when she started her okra farm and hauled her truck load of okra to the officials at the county seat, trying to persuade them to change the vegetable of the county. Opal Mae said they all were impressed with Iona's haul and put her on public television for a while, but the show never did catch on and even though it had a catchy little title she supposed folks just weren't interested in The Okra Show. Euna slammed down her fork, and we all stopped talking. She turned to Juna and said Reverend Gaddis never asked anyone to marry him but me, Euna Louise Finch. Opal Mae tried to change the subject again and asked Hilmer what was so interesting in the Sunday paper since he wasn't participating in the conversation. Hilmer said she'd gone too far with it this time and we all leaned in even closer than before as he read the headline out loud: Local Resident Abducted By Aliens. Last Tuesday evening, local resident Miss Baby Faye Bennett of the Bennett family that owns the 'Stoned Forever' rock quarry, claims she was transported from her bed to an alien spacecraft. She said the experience was unusual and only unpleasant when they attached a metal device to her head and though she didn't think it would leave a scar she hated for anyone to see her without her wig. Juna said 'course how could it have been unpleasant since she's got the hardest head in town. Hilmer said it says right here in the Sunday newspaper that she was levitated up into the spacecraft and the aliens were mighty sociable and asked her if there was anyone else like her and she said, why yes, yes indeed, there's a whole town full of us down below. She said the next thing she knew she was back in her bed. Hilmer said the article goes on to say that she would be proud to be the point of contact between heavenly bodies and—Euna interrupted and said she remembered back when Baby Faye loved to be the point of contact between anybody and the sheets. Hilmer laughed and started to say something when everyone started blurting out comments over comments…a whisper of a town…diverse with personality…stop talking so much…wouldn't be a bad thing. We all laughed as the bells of the clock tower told the late afternoon hour. We all agreed to meet next Sunday after church.

The Shelf

One day I took my heart out

And put it on a shelf

To save for a better time when there would be no doubt.

Another day I turned around

And saw you standing there amidst grace and love

profound

Each day with you eclipse the past

Our spirits collide and stars galore multiply

My heart found love at last

The Love Letter

Dear Ernie,

I found the perfect spot under a tree to write you this letter. The spot offered a lush place to linger, so I sat down. I felt close to you. We always enjoyed being outside, either walking through the woods, riding horses on the ranch, or sitting on the back porch watching Skipper chase the squirrels.

You left so suddenly I didn't have a chance to say good-bye. There was so much I wanted to say, but time seemed to overtake us—time spent opening shades, closing shutters, sweeping floors, and arranging quilts and pillows, oblivious to the minutes ticking away. That speeding train of life that seemed to move faster and faster down the track, playing hide and seek with clues of the future. We didn't pay attention.

Now I have you captured by this pen and paper. I can write down the memories and shape the sequence of words into visual paintings from my heart and lay them to rest right here. I knead and stroke our memories until the best parts rise up in perfect form and harmony and finally lapse into perfect folds in my mind. I remember the best. You are the best.

We saw each other for the first time our freshman year in high school in the cafeteria. I looked at you looking at me from across the room. You were talking with a friend, but you never took your eyes off me. I learned later that you were telling your friend to look at the girl with the blonde ponytail because she was going to be your girlfriend.

I fell in love with you that day. I read somewhere that falling in love was like falling asleep. For me, the feeling was like a punch in the stomach. And somehow I knew you felt that same punch that day. The universe aligned our souls, and I am grateful for the happiness it gave me to love you.

I still remember the way you used to ride your bicycle into my front yard, jumping off mid-peddle and letting it roll into the hydrangeas. You hopped off, grinning from ear-to-ear, proud of your boyish feat. You were my hero, and I grinned from ear-to-ear as well.

I'll be peeling an apple and suddenly remember our college homecoming football game. You bought me a candy apple on a stick. I was about to take a giant bite when our quarterback intercepted the football. The entire crowd exploded into a frenzied mob. We jumped up and threw our arms into the air with a collective purpose of willing the quarterback to run faster.

When I brought my arms back down the only thing left in my hand was an empty stick. The candy apple had launched into orbit with an unknown destination, landing site, or timing of touchdown. You bit your bottom lip, trying not to laugh. I had little power other than to burst out laughing myself. I jumped into your arms, wrapped my arms around your neck and shouted, "I love you—I love you!" And then you planted a huge kiss in the cove of my neck as the quarterback ran sixty yards for the winning touchdown. I will never forget the moment.

Our saving grace that day was that no one asked over the PA system if there was a doctor in the stadium to attend to a candy apple-wounded bystander. When I think about it today I still giggle.

I will always remember the last time we were at Landa Park Springs and the pavilion. It was late fall and we were the only ones there. We planned it that way. You flipped the switch to the lights that were draped in, out, and around the limbs of pecan trees situated around the dance floor. Several light bulbs hissed and cracked because of constant use during the summer. Shards of light bulbs fell to the dance floor, dimming the light surrounding us so moonlight could shine through.

We stood a few feet apart. You walked up and cupped my face in your hands. I met your gaze and took a breath that triggered the attention of my senses and made me think that I could fly to the moon. Without saying a word, you slipped your arms to my waist and our bodies swayed in place, moving our feet over the dance floor, sounding as if dancing on sand. We moved slowly in a circle, a half-circle, a quarter circle, and then the only movement came from our hearts—each beat strong and vital for the other. I was dreaming awake.

You kissed me. I welcomed you and pressed my body against you, trying to make us one. You moved your lips randomly up and down and around the terrain of my neck and shoulders.

Then, you took my hand and held my arm out suspended mid-air as you moved, kiss by kiss, up my arm as passage to my lips. Your tongue circled my lips and seduced my tongue into your mouth. Waves of weakness ricocheted through my body as my knees grew weak. We had kissed many times, but this kiss was alive, artistic. I felt safe in your arms. I felt safe in your movements and in your love.

The wind whipped around us and scattered leaves everywhere, making crisp little sounds like tap dancers on the dance floor. The leaves played around our feet—orange, yellow, and red—like confetti in celebration of our love. It was quiet other than the crickets clicking and an occasional owl breaking the silence with his haunting refrain—"h-o-o h-o-o...h-o-o h-o-o." I thought, you, you, you.

I feared I might fall to my knees when your fingers played with my hair like strands of silk at the back of my neck. Your fingers encouraged my surrender as another gust of wind whipped around us. I shivered. Faster than the wind, you wrapped your arms around me like a blanket. You held me close. I felt safe and warm.

I smelled the collar of your washed and pressed shirt.

I wanted to have been the one to have washed and pressed it. Mist began to fall. The smell of your collar blended with the smell of your skin made me feel as if I was being bathed in a rainforest. I imagined the smells of the earth filling each raindrop with its essence—ocean mist, honeycomb, mint leaves, dog's breath, river sand, and lemons. It was a simple memory, forever alive and cherished over the years. I kept you close with ease.

I am saying good-bye now—leaving you—but in some ways still can't ever, won't ever accept this. I want to be in your arms again so badly, but I know that harboring wishes and dreams don't always make wishes and dreams come true. I've never known such heartache and pain; I didn't realize a broken heart could continue limping along, drowning amidst memories that were born and raised by each of us.

I hear thunder in the distance. I will gather up my writing materials and reluctantly give up my writing nest. I will walk a few yards and stop at your gravesite. I will lay the yellow rose at your headstone, still not accepting this as the end.

The final dissection of my heart is complete. Dissection is a word with edges that slice deeply, with no hint of repair or healing. The remnants of my broken heart will speak forever of its loss.

I will remember two things in my life that are true: your love, and that when the world turns upside-down and

I fall, I know you will be there to catch me.

I will be with you always, Suzanne

You and Me

I can be what I am

When I am with you

I am what can be

When I am me

With you.

About the Author

Suzanne Mason is a storyteller and author who lives in Alexandria, VA. She grew up in Texas Hill Country, where much of her inspiration is rooted. *A Crack in the Sidewalk* is her second book. Her first book, *Be Still My Heart*, is available on BarnesandNoble.com.

Once you love

whatever the ending

A little remains

broken heart unmending

www.ingramcontent.com/pod-product-compliance
Lightning Source LLC
Chambersburg PA
CBHW070549310726
48982CB00011B/1517/J

* 9 7 8 0 9 8 1 8 5 9 7 5 0 *